BIRTHDAY WISHES AND MURDER

A Fiona Fleming Cozy Novella

PATTI LARSEN

CHAPTER ONE

Who would have thought I'd be turning the big two-nine in a small local pub decorated most tackily for the pending Halloween spooktacular three weeks ahead in paper pumpkins and cutout garlands? In my old hometown, no less, when only six short months ago I imagined partying in booming pubs in downtown Manhattan?

Life, my friend. It's like that, yo.

Mind you, I would likely have been locked in my tiny apartment I'd rented after finding out my long-term boyfriend had cheated rather than living it up with all the friends who abandoned me after I called him out, eating ice cream in my pajamas and crying over the years I wasted if things had gone differently. Instead, I found myself entering the Harp and Thorn on Reading's main street, the attempt at a Tudor-style pub in the cutest town in America (according to our mayor's tourism campaign) the closest thing we had to a happening spot this side of Montpelier.

Vermont. Such a happening place.

Now, don't get me wrong. My life had changed so much for the better since I'd come home to my tiny mountain town, despite the facts of the past. Losing my Grandmother Iris meant inheriting her bed and breakfast, Petunia's, along with her very fat and farty pug of the same name. But it also meant reconnecting with my parents after ten years living away, as well as my best friend, Daisy Bruce. The very person who had invited me out to this particular party of two, her beaming smile, honey-blonde mass of curls and giant, sparkling gray eyes as authentic as her bubbling personality made it very hard to say no.

Don't read anything into my attitude, please. I wasn't anti-birthday or anything, to the contrary, typically. But this single spin around the sun shy of a new decade had me thinking about what I'd accomplished in my life so far and coming up short on satisfaction.

"Let's sit at the bar." Daisy dragged me toward the far side of the establishment, two open stools at the end the only empty seats available. I'd have preferred a table, but Day acted like the remaining spots were the best ones in the house. I really needed to absorb some more of her happy-go-lucky optimism, because the idea of spending my 29th at the end of a packed bar surrounded by loud locals and tourists was feeling like an epic letdown.

Far from Daisy's fault, but there you had it.

"Two margaritas, Patrick." My bestie's breathless giggle followed her order, her deep red wool coat sliding from her narrow shoulders, the 50s swing dress beneath matching the shade. Day's sense of style had forced me to push myself to at least try to make an effort, though these days wearing my hair down instead of in a messy bun of unruly red curls and donning a skirt and blouse when jeans and a t-shirt were my uniform at Petunia's was about as far as I made it in the fancy-pants department.

The Harp and Thorn's owner, Patrick Huss, blinked at Daisy like she'd spoken a foreign language before trundling off to make our drinks, his staff maneuvering around him with expert ease, hustling while the tipsy bartender sampled more of his own wares before getting to ours. While I'd inherited messy guests and a fragrant dog, Patrick had come into more of his favorite pastime through his father, his high school habit unchanged.

Which had me sighing before I could stop myself because nothing really *had* changed since I'd left Reading, had it? And what did my coming home with nothing but an Arts degree I didn't use, and a broken heart really have to say about my own personal growth?

Daisy's instant concern had my guilt at the ready. Before she could ask, gorgeous face falling into a worried expression, I patted her hand with a forced smile.

"Thanks for this," I said, doing my best not to ruin her night, too, while internally kicking myself for my terrible attitude. "It's going to be fun." It was, darn it.

It *was*.

Daisy hugged me quickly before letting me go with a softer smile that still lit her face despite the reduced wattage. "I know it's not New York," she said.

"Thankfully," I told her with a firm tone. Paused a little while I drew a slow breath, then tried to articulate what I was feeling. "Do you ever wonder if you missed the train, Day? That you're meant for something, and you just didn't find it?" Yup, that was it. Talk about doom and gloom, why don't ya?

My best friend nodded, curls bouncing over one shoulder, gray gaze direct and a little sad. "I know exactly what you mean." That just made me feel like a total jerk, especially since I knew very well Daisy had been bopping from one thing to another, this job to that career option since I'd left Reading. Her present assistance at my bed and breakfast was honestly the most amazing thing that could have happened to me, but I was aware it might be temporary. Before I could apologize for bringing down our vibe, however, Day brightened, her whole being beaming. "Maybe it just means we have our things to look forward to, Fee. How wonderful is that? We're old enough to appreciate them when they come along, right?"

Her outlook was so freaking delightful I found

myself smiling in return. Because Fiona Fleming? You were not going to drag Daisy into doldrums when she deserved better.

"Right," I said, accepting my drink from a server, clinking the frozen strawberry concoction with my bestie.

"Happy birthday to the most amazing best friend ever." Daisy gushed as she warbled that line, shoulders rising, adorable smile wrinkling her nose. "Here's to all the birthdays together until we're old ladies laughing over all the awesome we've done."

I could have hugged her again, I really could. She made everything so much better. Trouble was, we weren't alone in the bar, were we? And not everyone was welcome in our little celebration.

Tell that to the guy sitting next to her who leaned in with a grin and a lingering stare for my best friend's ample chest that instantly triggered my redheaded protectiveness and shifted me from my burgeoning good mood to cranky again. "Hey, gorgeous," he said, holding up his beer. "It's my birthday, too." Um, okay, whatever, bro. "You hotties want to celebrate together?"

Hard pass. Now to convince him I meant it.

CHAPTER TWO

I'd been hit on before, of course. There was a certain demographic of men who liked redheads despite our reputations (mine well earned) for the temperamental (no laughing). Thing was, I sort of expected it when I was out and about in a city as large as New York. It had been quite some time however since my return to Reading and my dry spell when it came to male attention. Considering the only man I'd felt even a remote bit of interest for happened to be our new town sheriff—the same sheriff who'd had me as his prime suspect in a murder I didn't commit only five months ago—I'd resigned myself to the fact I'd be leaning toward the spinsterly persuasion for the remainder of my long and sad life. Reading only had a small population of single men, after all, and I happened to be related to one of them.

Ew. Had I just grouped Robert Carlisle in with the tiny eligibility pool? Forgive me while I washed my brain out with gasoline and set myself on fire.

My disgusting cousin notwithstanding, you'd think under these circumstances I'd be wide open to a little male attention, right? Yeah, not this Fleming. Considering the breakup, I still raged over in the deep, dark night while running endless scenarios where my ex, Ryan Richards, died horrible deaths or endured cycles of browbeating that made him apologize wasn't doing much to encourage trust and faith in the male half of the race.

And from the smarmy look on our neighbor's face—not to mention the fact he was easily a decade older than us—he wasn't exactly a prize to be swooned over. Honestly, if he looked at Day's chest one more time, I was going to see what he looked like with margarita all over his face.

He wasn't alone either, the three men sitting in a row on his left side leaning in to see who he was harassing while I contemplated a short and pithy retort to his unwelcome question. They all appeared about the same age, maybe forty, our closest neighbor's dark hair liberally peppered with silver, hazel eyes a bit glossy, probably from excessive alcohol consumption. All four were well-dressed, likely on a boy's trip without their partners, too much time and too much money on their grasping little hands than was good for them. They might have been hoping for a stag trip to remember, but I wasn't into mid-life crisis management, thanks.

Daisy beat me to it in classic fashion, blinking those huge, beautiful eyes, full lips pulling back into a dazzling smile that had him leaning toward her even further while she giggled a little.

"Happy birthday," she said. "Fifty this year?"

His three friends spluttered before bursting into laughter that had their friend blanching white while I bit my lower lip to keep from hee-hawing a donkey bray of appreciation for my best friend's delivery. See, the thing about Daisy was you just couldn't get mad at her. She had this authentic way of kindness and brilliance that disarmed even the most aggressive soul. So, while I knew it had to cut deep—sure, he was older, but no way he was *that* much older—he accepted her question without a cutting remark in return.

If it had been me? No way I'd have gotten away with it. But Day?

Slam freaking dunk for the win.

He backed off instantly, turning to his friends without a word, shoulder turned toward Daisy. She carried on like it was no biggie, while I slow-clapped silently in appreciation for her class.

"I'm buying the next one," I said. "Just for that."

She winked a long, slow wink, lashes brushing her cheek. Speaking of cheek, if she grinned any tighter, she'd pop a tooth.

Neither of us got to appreciate the moment for long, however, as the front door of the pub slammed open, and a small blonde woman stormed through. I only noted her entry because of the sound of the door thudding against the wall, and I wasn't the only one to turn with an eyebrow raised to watch her stomp her way across the floor. The four men didn't seem to notice, not until she grasped birthday boy by the shoulder and spun him, the stool obliging her despite the size he had over her, to face her, his expression shifting from shock to sullen resentment even as she faced him down with fury on her overly-made-up face.

"You think I wouldn't know what you did, Davis?" She tossed her heavily highlighted hair over the shoulder of her white coat, cheeks pink either from the cool October evening air or her anger or both. "How dare you?"

He grumbled something while one of his companions, the man furthest from him, slipped from his stool and tried to intervene. "Lora," he said in a deep voice, bald head catching the light, the flash of an expensive gold and diamond ring on his right hand reinforcing my earlier assessment while the blonde cut him off with a sharp chop of her hand in his general direction as her furious gaze never left the birthday boy.

"Stay out of this, Adam." She jabbed a French manicured finger into the first man's chest. "This is between me and my husband."

"Ex-husband," one of the other men muttered, falling silent when she shot him a furious look.

"We'll talk about this when I get back to

Montpelier," Davis grumbled. "You're not welcome here, Lora."

"I want my money," she snarled in his face, shaking in rage, puffy lower lip trembling, hands clenched at her sides while her heavy makeup sank deep into the line between her brows as she scowled. "You won't get away with this."

"My money," Davis said, spinning back toward the bar with a wave over his shoulder, downing the last of his drink and waving at Patrick for a refill. "Go home before you embarrass yourself further."

"*Embarrass* myself?" She almost shrieked those two words before pulling herself together. "You cheated on me, Davis Zaine. You're the one who humiliated himself." She grasped for his arm to turn him around again, only to have him jerk himself free, half-lunging for her with a furious look on his face.

Okay, so I probably should have stayed out of it because she seemed to be imploding without any help and whatever was between them wasn't any of my business. And there were more than enough people around to defend her if he did end up physical, his own friends turning to grab for him. Yup, I might have held my tongue if it had been any other circumstance. But the fresh wound my ex, Ryan inflicted on me? Cut deep enough to trigger my temper in Lora Zaine's favor and had me spinning my stool toward them, scowling at the cheating ex-husband over my now shocked and staring best friend.

"Dude," I said, reaching out and nabbing the

sleeve of his jacket before he could stand, "you put one hand on her, and I'll have you arrested."

He glowered at me, sinking back into his stool. "Don't touch me." He was clearly on the verge of too drunk to know what was best for him, because the man he'd called Adam tried to talk to him in a low tone, but Davis simply pushed him away with enough force the bald man bounced into one of their other friends while Lora backed off a half-step with one hand over her mouth.

"Not in my bar." Patrick might have been in the sauce himself, but he wasn't about to see it trashed, was he?

"Sorry about this," Adam said, smile beaming over the counter at Patrick even as a bill slipped across the surface. I caught sight of Benjamin Franklin gently smiling up at the barkeep and knew immediately Adam was singing the ballad of Patrick's people. "Lora," he turned back to the woman, smile now strained, "Davis is just blowing off some steam this weekend. Go back to Montpelier and I'll make sure you two get to talk."

"I'm not going anywhere, Adam," she snarled in return, her momentary surprise vanquished. "Not until Davis releases my half of the money." She jabbed for her ex again before Adam could stop her. "I'll sue you for everything for this."

It was obviously time to get out of there. Other people's drama might have been entertaining on a TV show, but I wasn't all that keen about being part of it while struggling with my self-worth and present living situation. But as I reached for Daisy with a nod for the door, Davis made a foolish, foolish move that cemented the outcome of our encounter.

As my bestie slid down from her stool, he noticed. And grabbed for her, tugging her to him while Day's eyes flew wide. "We're here to have fun," he slurred at his ex-wife. "You're ruining the party." And then, before Daisy could react, he leaned in to kiss her.

So, I mentioned my temper, right?

Yeah.

Um.

Yeah.

Daisy was perfectly capable of taking care of herself and was in process of doing just that when my brain exploded in rage, and I reached out almost casually and cuffed the idiot across the ear like I swatted a fly.

Now, don't get me wrong. I didn't condone violence, not on the worst of days. In fact, the idea of hitting anyone was just that—an idea. I'd had enough confrontations in my life thanks to my temper, of course, but none of them had ended in me actually striking someone, not even Ryan or the bimbo I'd found in my bed. Correction, I'd landed a solid punch once, at the tender age of eleven, again in defense of the gorgeous woman next to me, though the bully girl who'd taken the hit had been my size, not a hulking brute of a baby who was supposed to be an adult and know freaking better.

Yup, this was different. And apparently, I had a

soft spot when it came to Daisy, my amazing and loving and caring friend who didn't deserve to be treated like a piece of meat in the rough and callous grip of a cheating liar and thief who clearly had boundary and possession issues.

So, I hit him. Sure did. No regrets, either. Not even when, the very moment the loud smack echoed in the now quiet of the bar as everyone turned to stare, I realized two familiar men—the last two men on the planet I'd have wanted to witness my moment of anger—stood at the front door watching the drama unfold.

One of them? My vile cousin, Deputy Robert Carlisle, if only because it was weakness and he'd do everything in his power to hold it against me for the rest of my life. The other? Even more devastating, though I wasn't sure why except the fact the delicious creature who was Sheriff Crew Turner? Made me wish I could crawl under a rock from the surprise and flash of disappointment on his face.

Well, craptastic.

CHAPTER THREE

The same moment I noticed the two men in uniform, Davis spotted them too. And instantly reacted while still clinging to the now red-faced Daisy. "Officers! Arrest this woman for assault!"

Um, okay, jerkface. I couldn't have been the only person there who gaped in disbelief, right? Because the idiot had his hands on my best friend still, didn't he?

Not for long. I have no idea what she did, but with a solid grunt Davis released Daisy like she'd burned him despite the fact whatever it was she'd pulled off, she managed to get him to let her go without any kind of active accusation, so I guess I needed to learn more things from her in the future.

Before I got arrested.

Crew joined us, scowling like he always seemed to in my presence, though his focus appeared to be on Davis, not me for once. "Ms. Bruce," he said, not even looking at Daisy, "can I assume this gentleman acted without your permission?"

"You can, sheriff," my bestie said in a prim voice, smoothing the front of her dress with an arched eyebrow. "But I won't be pressing charges. I'm sure he's seen the error of his ways."

Davis was rubbing at his ribcage and glaring at her all the while.

"Mr...?" Crew waited for the offender to answer, Robert lurking behind him with that 70s pornstache he seemed to think attractive wriggling on his upper lip, pot belly protruding just enough over his belt it bulged out the waistband of his puffy uniform coat. Whether he meant to offer himself up as backup or not (likely not, knowing Robert, only there because he wanted in on the drama), the effect was the same. But not on the offender.

"Sheriff, Adam Carson." The bald friend interceded before the birthday boy could speak up, fixed smile and firm handshake he offered to Crew clearly practiced and likely necessary more than once in the past, though it had me wondering why someone would step up for a creep like Davis. "Please, forgive us for the kerfuffle. It's Davis's birthday and we're celebrating."

Crew's expression didn't soften. "Mr...?" He repeated that question to the offender who finally mumbled, "Zaine," in response. "Mr. Zaine." He glanced at me, the tic under his eye twitching just a little, enough I knew he'd have words for me later but chose otherwise at the moment. "You do realize manhandling another person without their permission is also assault."

Davis spluttered while his bald friend let out a little laugh, one hand firmly pressed to the other man's chest. "Of course, we won't be pressing charges," he said.

Daisy cocked her head to one side, sweet smile on her face. "That's a smart decision," she said ever-so brightly. "I'd hate to have to change my mind, after all."

Davis sat back, shrugged. "Just being friendly."

"I'm sure." Crew finally turned and met my eyes, expression unchanged. "Ms. Fleming," he said, "perhaps it would be best if you and Ms. Bruce found somewhere else to sit."

He did *not* just say anything of the sort. "Why should *we* move?" Oh, I had a head of steam on and he just misogynized himself into my black books with his little suggestion.

"It's all right, Fee," Day said, a soft touch to my arm not helping matters.

"It's *not*." I stood and faced off with Crew Turner, shocked at his lack of protection for locals. Had he fallen into the whole tourism mentality our mayor, Olivia Walker, had layered on so thick it made me choke? "Two women have every right to sit at a bar and have a drink without some strange drunk guy being free with his hands. And you know it." Crew's jaw jumped, blue eyes troubled. "If anyone needs to leave, it's *them*." I jabbed an index finger in the foursome's direction, noting the ex-wife hovered on the periphery, smirking at Davis's obvious discomfort.

Crew took a slow, even breath, dark hair peeking out from under his knitted cap, his wide jaw clenched against whatever it was he was feeling—annoyance, frustration, the need to shake me, you decide—before responding. "If Daisy won't press charges, there's nothing I can do." He said it quietly, directly to me, deep voice growling just a little. "So, make my life easier, please, Ms. Fleming, and find another place to sit."

"No need," Adam interrupted, nodding to me and then to Daisy. "My deepest apologies for Davis and his actions. Here," he gently guided his friend to the seat he'd been using on the far side of their other two companions before taking the stool Davis vacated himself. Then, he raised both hands in front of him as though to show he was harmless. "I'll personally vouch for his behavior going forward. My apologies to you, Ms. Bruce, Ms. Fleming, for any discomfort."

Lora Zaine snorted as she shoved her way into the circle again. "You're a better friend than he ever deserved, Adam," she snarled. "Why you even bother I have no idea."

"And you are?" Crew turned to her while Robert aimed an index finger and thumb at me and pulled his imaginary trigger, grinning like this whole situation was highly amusing to him. Soured my mood further, believe it, and had me thinking leaving was a good idea after all.

"Lora Zaine," the blonde said. "The unfortunate former wife of that piece of work." She jabbed a thumb over one shoulder, her white designer coat swinging, heavy leather purse banging against her side as she did. "You're sure you don't want to arrest him?"

Crew flashed a little, grim smile. "Not yet," he said. "But the night is young. I don't want to get any calls about this, Mr. Carson," he told Adam. "Don't make me regret my decision to let this go."

"Of course, sheriff," the bald man said with a smile and a nod.

Crew paused like he wanted to say more before sighing and shaking his head. He did stop one last moment to bend close to Daisy, whispering something I couldn't hear, my bestie shaking her head with a dimpled grin he seemed to accept before he turned and strode out.

I wish Robert had gone with him. Instead, my revolting cousin took a turn at me while his boss headed for the door.

"If I were sheriff you'd be in cuffs by now." He snorted long and deep while I cringed at the sound and fought off nausea. "Watch yourself, Fanny." Robert flashed Daisy a gross grin, that monstrous mustache of his not doing him any favors. He might have been our age, but Robert's thinning, straight haircut paired with his facial fur choice didn't flatter him any more than his sunken eyes did.

Not to mention his attitude.

The thing was, though, his snarky attack had succeeded where Daisy's request to stay would have failed because you can bet your bottom dollar there was no way I was leaving the Harp and Thorne until the four men in question did.

It was now a matter of principle, and I was a dog with a bone.

"We're really sorry about that." One of the other men leaned across Adam, his earnest expression softening my attitude a little. "Davis isn't always like this. He's just blowing off some steam."

The fourth friend eye-rolled as he turned his back to the birthday boy now arguing in a hissing match with his ex-wife further down the bar. "Don't listen to Jamie here," he said, highlighted hair perfectly styled, pale green eyes winking. "Davis is a jerk on the best of days. But we're nothing like him, right?" He elbowed the man beside him who shrugged before offering me his hand.

"Jamie Myles," he said. "You met Adam," the bald man beside me nodded vaguely, his gaze locked instead on the argument between the ex-spouses, focus of attention there to a level that had me wondering why he cared so much. "And this is Mac Dillon. Don't let his flirting bother you. He's not worth it."

I didn't get to respond, not when Davis suddenly erupted again with a nasty, "I'm done!" to Lora before he heaved himself off the stool and headed for the back end of the bar and the bathrooms. She followed in a hurry, Adam sliding from his own stool to pursue while Jamie and Mac both shrugged and finished their drinks in a single swallow before going after them.

"I'm sorry," Daisy said, drawing my attention back to her, the moisture in her eyes and clear distress on her lovely face triggering guilt. "This was supposed to be fun for you. Did you want to go?"

I instantly shook my head and waved at Patrick. "No freaking way," I said, forcing a smile. "We're here to celebrate, Day. As long as you're okay, I'm staying."

She clinked glasses with me, sighing her relief. "You're the best, Fee."

She had no idea, did she?

Jamie returned first, ordering a drink before Mac returned. Adam finally came back as well, though there was no sign of Lora or Davis. Instead of dealing with them—Mac's further flirting attempts only annoyed me—I invited Daisy for a round of darts that had us both laughing and squealing for the next hour.

I hadn't realized how tired I was until I polished off my last margarita and let out a jaw-cracking yawn. Daisy instantly set aside her darts and took my glass from me, depositing both on the bar and fetching our coats.

"Sorry, Day," I said, tucking myself into mine and doing up the buttons, my bestie wrapping my scarf around my neck like I was her kid she was

22

mothering. "I don't mean to cut the night short."

"You're not," she insisted. "I know how busy you've been at Petunia's. I'm just glad we got this chance to come out for your birthday." Daisy hugged me. "I have a present for you back at your place." She pinked a little before clasping her hands in front her, a vision in a red beret and flared wool coat. "I hope you like it!"

I hooked my arm through hers and guided her toward the back door. "I know I'll love it," I said. "Thanks, Day. For everything." Wait, was I tearing up? I really *was* tired.

Or something.

Rather than exit the front, I took the back exit into the rear parking lot, the shortcut across to the next street then a straight shot to Petunia's. Daisy came with me, the two of us still linked at the elbow, her chatter about upcoming guests distracting me while the puffing mist of her warm breath floated between us. The moon had risen over the edge of the towering line of mountains, the crystal-clear night chill but still in the shelter of the valley. There were times I asked myself what I'd been thinking coming back here like this. And other times, like that moment of perfection when the whole world seemed to stand still to listen to Daisy talk that I knew I was where I was meant to be.

All of that crashed down around me as I glanced to my left on our way through the lot, a dark lump beside one of the parked cars catching my attention and making me pause. Even as I recognized a gloved hand lying on the pavement just before I broke free of Daisy and ran to investigate.

She was right on my heels, the pair of us stopping in shock to stare down into the glazed and empty eyes of the man spreadeagled on the ground, wide, silent gaze locked on nothing, mouth agape as if in surprise at his predicament.

Davis Zaine just had his last birthday.

CHAPTER FOUR

I huddled inside my coat, Daisy at my side, while Sheriff Crew Turner wrote down everything I told him. His arrival upon our call to alert him of the dead body had been met with a heavy sigh and his expression upon landing back at the bar, this time with Robert and his second deputy, Jill Wagner in tow, had exasperation dominating. When I instantly attempted to explain I wasn't responsible, however, he waved off my words with a head shake.

"I know you didn't do it," he said, looking down at the body. "But why is it, Ms. Fleming, you seem to have this need to complicate my life?"

Like mine wasn't complicated, too, thank you. Regardless of his opinions of my luck or otherwise, Crew handled the situation with the level of professionalism and thoroughness I'd come to expect from him, asking questions and accepting my answers, Daisy's add-ons no less respected, while our local ME arrived to take possession of the corpse of Davis Zaine.

All before anyone inside could find out something was up. Though that wasn't going to last long, considering as Dr. Lloyd Aberstock bent over the prone figure of the deceased, the door to the pub's rear entrance opened, discharging a few customers. They all stopped in shock at the sight of police tape and the doc in his white marshmallow coverall before they ducked back inside.

Crew's second sigh had a sound of defeat to it. "This is about to turn into a circus," he said. "Anything else you need to tell me before the entirety of this town's population shows up to make me miserable?"

I knew very well our mayor had her own opinions about how her new sheriff should be handling cases and that first and foremost was her desire to protect Reading's reputation. Which meant she had been rather heavy-handed with the man who took over from my father. And while retired Sheriff John Fleming wouldn't have put up with Olivia's domineering (possibly the reason Dad retired from the position after decades of service), Crew didn't seem to have the reputation built up yet to get his way. I did feel for him, honestly. It couldn't have been easy to take this job, not following in the footsteps of my father, Reading's beloved former sheriff. Nor to handle Olivia and her hyper-focused drive to put our town on the map. Still, his attitude made me frown even as his prophecy came true, and the back door of the pub suddenly disgorged what looked like the entire selection of patrons and staff.

Robert might have been useless and did more gawking at the body than his actual job, but Jill was on the ball, holding back the onlookers single-handedly with the kind of grit and determination that had me glaring at my cousin until he slumped off to help her. Leaving me with Crew, Daisy still hanging onto my arm, while Dr. Aberstock joined us.

The adorable man who always reminded me of Santa Claus beamed a lovely smile in my direction, including Daisy in his murmured greeting, the charming Dr. Aberstock nodding to Crew as he pushed the elastic hood from his silver hair, beard popping free when he undid the zipper, blue eyes sparkling and cheeks that cherub pink that seemed to hint at a solid Ho, Ho, Ho.

"Blunt force trauma," he said. "Looks like a traumatic brain injury, but I'll know more when I conduct the autopsy. Are you all right, Fee? Daisy?" Dr. Aberstock had stripped his gloves as the two EMTs started zipping Davis Zaine into a body bag, gurney at the ready, the lights of the ambulance turned off on Crew's request. Not that it did any good now with the patrons gaping and a woman's voice piercing the cold air nearby. I didn't have to look to know it was Lora Zaine, the words muffled but her emotional outburst clear enough.

"We're okay, Dr. Aberstock," I said.

"You let me know if either of you need anything," he said, squeezing Daisy's hand before saluting Crew with a cheeky gesture. "I'll let you get to your job while I do mine. Sheriff, ladies." He joined the EMTs, just starting to zip up the bag when footsteps turned all of us around, Lora Zaine racing over the asphalt toward us. Crew caught her just in time, the three men her ex-husband had come to Reading with on her heels, Lora stopping in her tracks while Crew stepped in her way. It was obvious from the shock on her face, the sudden wash of grief that it wasn't the sheriff's intervention that made her freeze, however. With a wail of agony, she collapsed forward, Adam Carson catching her from behind, the other two men joining him to help support her while Dr. Aberstock grimly finished zipping the body bag closed before the EMTs loaded the whole shebang onto the gurney.

"Davis, no!" Lora sobbed, almost incoherent, those two words the only ones I made out as she fought for breath. She'd had a solid hate on not so long ago, but I guess I could understand grief, especially if there was enough unresolved emotion between them.

Would I have wept if I found Ryan dead?

Snort. Sorry. Carrying on.

"What happened?" Adam's disbelief and shock matched his friends, though my mind couldn't help but come to a conclusion, could it? Because I had this thing about minding my own business.

"I'm investigating that right now," Crew said. "For now, I'm sorry for your loss. If you'll come with me, I have questions for you about Mr. Zaine's death I need you to answer."

"Was he murdered?" That was Mac, his flirting ways long gone in the face of death.

"Are we suspects?" Jamie was the first to back up, shaking his head, both hands raised in front of him, expression settling into grim unease. "I didn't have anything to do with it."

Lora blinked, her sobbing slowing as she looked back and forth between Jamie and Crew before blurting, "Murder?"

"If you'll all please come with me." The sheriff's lack of patience with me didn't seem to translate to the four suspects. Oh, you better believe I was looking at them. If it was murder. Which I instantly jumped to right along with the others. "We don't have any answers yet. I just need to ask you some questions." He waved at Jill who joined us. "Please escort Mr. Zaine's companions to the office, Deputy Wagner."

"Right away, sheriff." Her blonde ponytail stuck oddly out from under her knit cap, but there was nothing amusing about tall, broad-shouldered and soft-spoken Jill Wagner. "Follow me, please."

They did, if hesitantly, and I hardly blamed them. Especially if one or more had something to do with Davis's death. Which had my mind spinning and must have shown on my face.

How did I know that? Crew leaned in toward me,

voice very low as he spoke, deep blue eyes locked on mine and body positioned to block my view of the departing suspects. Mourners. Whatever.

"Thank you for the call," he said. "I'm sure I don't have to *again*," yes, he stressed that word while I harrumphed over it, "explain to the *former*," boy had to stop with the obvious, "sheriff's *daughter*," he was asking for a smackdown, I swear, "that nothing past this moment is any of your business and if I need anything at all, *I'll* call *you*." I glared while he paused, jaw jumping. "Agreed?"

I had every opportunity to do just that. Walk away without another word, just nod and mind my own business. I should have. I wanted to, really. Okay, don't believe me, but it's true. Thing was that my mouth and my brain always had this kind of tug-of-war situation that happened when someone of authority tried to boss me around. I blame my dad, but that was for another day and some talk therapy to explore.

So, that being said, you'll be understanding with me when my lips parted of their own accord and words emerged that I had zero control over.

"The ex-wife claimed he tried to rip her off," I said. "And the best friend seemed far too protective of him." I choked myself into a halt as Crew's face tightened, the vein in the middle of his forehead rising to pulse while the tic under his eye sped up a bit.

"I said," he growled, "*agreed?*"

Well, fine. You don't have to be such a jerk about

it.

It was Daisy who led me away with a chirping, "Agreed!" I went with her only because I was done anyway, grumbling under my breath the whole walk back to Petunia's while my best friend did her best to soothe my simmering temper.

"He's just doing his job," she said before wincing on the front steps to the bed and breakfast while I spun on her with hurt shock. "Sorry, Fee. It's not fair, I know. But he *is* sheriff, and this is his responsibility. Right?" She bit her lower lip, visible anxiety knocking the stuffing out of my anger and making me capitulate. Because nothing could calm me down like feeling I'd hurt my sweet and compassionate best friend over something I really needed to back down from.

"I know, Day," I said, sighing deeply while the zinging energy of my temper finally subsided and drained away. I looked up at the swinging sign over the white door of my business, cold air now affecting me, making me shiver without the heat of my blood boiling keeping me warm. "He just..."

She giggled a little, hugging me. "I know," she said, winking when she let me go. "You make each other crazy. Sounds like the beginning of something beautiful." She waved off my splutter of denial before hugging me one more time. "Happy birthday," she said. "I'll see you in the morning."

She was around the corner before I realized we'd both forgotten about the present she'd set aside for me. Not that I was in the mood for opening a gift right then, but the distraction might have helped. I went inside, the fat pug namesake of my B&B waddling her way from her station at the sideboard in the foyer, panting her joy at my appearance. I said goodnight to the girl I'd left in charge (Annie? Sophia? I sucked at names) before checking my messages. I groaned as I realized I'd forgotten dinner with my parents the next evening. Not that I didn't want to have birthday dinner with them. On the contrary. I'd loved reconnecting with them so deeply since I'd come back to Reading. But it would mean answering a million questions from Dad who, in my estimation, still loved and longed for life in law enforcement. And talking to Dad would lead to questions about the case and me annoying Crew because I wouldn't be able to stay out of it...

Hopefully, he'd wrap things up before my inner busybody made a nuisance of herself.

I drew a deep breath as I turned to lock up. The old house seemed to inhale itself as its quiet embraced me, the few guests I had in residence already tucked away and sleeping, my pug following me on her ticking claws (that yet again needed attention) over the hardwood floor, the soul of the house embracing me as it sometimes seemed to do, calming me the rest of the way until my weariness returned and drew out a long, deep yawn the pug mimicked.

"Bed, sweet girl," I said.

She grunted her agreement. Even as someone strode through the door like she owned the place instead of me.

Lora Zaine took one look at me and froze, face contorting. "You!"

CHAPTER FIVE

Whatever reason she had for firing off that one word like an accusation, she wasn't getting away with such an attitude in my place, thank you very much. I simply stared back, blank-faced and silent, giving her the opportunity to backpedal. Which she did, since it became clear to me she realized, as her gaze darted around the foyer of Petunia's, her night's rest relied on yours truly.

"Mrs. Zaine," I said at last. "You've already checked in, I take it?"

Her lack of luggage and the key dangling from one gloved hand said as much in tandem, but I wanted to ensure I drove the point home. It worked, the woman blanching under her white fur hat, pristine wool coat of the same color hugging her small frame in a tight embrace that made her look like a china doll.

"I have," she said. Stopped again, licking her lips, visibly shaken and struggling. Well, she did just lose her ex-husband to unknown circumstances, so I figured I'd cut her some slack.

"I'm very sorry for your loss," I said. "If there's anything I or my staff can do to make your stay more comfortable, please let me know."

She bobbed a nod while the door behind her opened again and three men I instantly recognized walked inside. All three fell silent from their chatter, the cold air they allowed to whisk its way across the floor to chill me sending goosebumps up my arms, almost as much as the vaguely uncomfortable and rather guilty set of expressions on each of the men's faces.

Did they know something about Davis Zaine's death I didn't?

"Gentlemen," I said. "Welcome to Petunia's." My pug hadn't moved from her place at my feet, oddly. Usually, the portly pooch liked to waddle her adorable way to meet guests, likely in the hope of snacks as much as pats. Tonight, either she was too tired to make the effort or something in her rather empty and kindly little mind registered that keeping her distance was her best bet. I took her reticence for the latter, though part of me fumed over the circumstance because I knew exactly who had sent the three men here.

And no, they didn't have a reservation.

"Ms. Fleming." Again it was Adam Carson who took the fore, his smile filling in the unhappy spaces he'd previously borne, coming forward to shake my hand. "Apologies, but Sheriff Turner asked us to stay in town until the medical examiner completes his autopsy."

Yup. Knew it. And you know what? If Crew Turner really did want me to keep my nose out of police business, he had a ridiculously frustrating way of showing it.

"Of course," I said, turning back to the sidebar, Petunia following close on my heels, sinking down to sit on one of my feet as I rebooted the computer and logged in.

It didn't take long to assign each of the men a room, sending them up to the third floor while Lora Zaine remained on the second. Not that I was trying to separate them, but I figured she'd have a more restful time of things if she didn't constantly run into her ex's three friends. I had my own unhappy history with men, after all, and while I tried not to let it influence me on the day-to-day, I felt myself now leaning toward empathy for her and not so much for the trio who lugged their bags (at 10PM at night? Better believe it) to their rooms.

She paused as they went up, joining me when I again turned off the computer then headed for the front door to lock it before anyone else could wander in and make my night more memorable than it already was.

"I know it's late," she said, looking suddenly frail

and far less antagonistic, face fallen into sorrow, lines pulling at the corners of her mouth and eyes, shoulders rounding forward inside her heavy coat. "But I don't think I could manage sleep just yet. Can I trouble you for some tea?"

"Right this way," I said, gesturing to the entry to the dining room, turning the light on for her. "I'll be right back."

It didn't take long to brew a pot, cream and sugar dishes loaded on a tray and Grandmother Iris's favorite china cups and saucers neatly stacked around. There had been a time I'd have been worried to invade the kitchen space without approval from my cook, Betty Jones or her sister, Mary, for that matter. We'd all come to a bit of an agreement, however, the elderly women who'd been here from day one no longer concerned I was going to fire them for some new-fangled upgrades. The opposite, it seemed. Their experience and presence now made my life easier instead of otherwise.

Old dogs and new tricks. And yes, I was the old dog, not them.

As for the second cup and saucer that joined the first, you can believe I was taking a sip of my own after the night I'd had. I set the tray down in front of Lora, noting she seemed even more petite than before, her tight jeans and sweater accentuating her delicateness, warmer attire set aside. Petunia's hesitation continued, the chubby pug parking herself beside me but without her characteristic flop and moan as she settled. Instead, she stood upright with her back legs straight out, front paws between them, huge eyes staring up at our guest as her black triangle ears perked in interest she rarely showed outside of offerings of food and love.

Lora ignored my dog, sighing softly over the cup of tea I poured her, one lump and a splash of cream preceding the tinkle of her stirring filling the room with the soft sound. I went for two lumps and enough of the white stuff to negate my tea, sitting back as Lora sipped and then sighed again, a soft puff of steam trailing up from the rim.

"Just what I needed, thank you." She took another drink before setting the cup down between her hands, the clink of it touching the saucer reminding me of my grandmother and this room, making me sad all over again and grateful she'd left me this place despite our distance the last ten years. Maybe it was my own lingering grief that had Lora open up to me, the emotional connection almost tactile between us in our shared moment of regret and sorrow. Or perhaps she just needed someone to talk to. Whatever her reason, she looked up at last, her blue eyes meeting mine as she forced a little smile. "He wasn't always such a..." Lora trailed off like she had a choice word or two stored up to use against her ex-husband before she shook her head and returned her gaze to her cup. "I met him when I was fourteen, imagine that." Her little laugh had an echo of old happiness in it, long fingernails making tapping sounds on the porcelain as she shifted her grip. Somewhere along the line, she seemed to have lost one of her gels, her right index finger bare. "We married young, had two kids. I stayed home, and he built his business. We had it all, a nice house, a great life. I thought our lives were perfect." They certainly sounded like the average middle-class American family. "Then, all of a sudden, a year ago he tells me he's been having an affair and wants a divorce, no conversation, no nothing." She dashed at sudden tears that escaped, dropping to the tablecloth. "The kids were devastated, and I didn't know what to do. I haven't had a day job since college." I nodded, feeling terrible for her. What a jerk. "Adam said it was a mid-life crisis. I worried Davis had a stroke." I couldn't help the tiny snort of amusement that emerged. Lora looked up, startled, then laughed herself. "I know, I'm terrible. But honestly."

"I'm so sorry," I said. "And now this."

She bobbed a heavy nod. "What will I tell the children?"

I didn't have an answer for that. "Mr. Carson seemed very concerned," I said, internally wincing because I was poking my nose in under the guise of compassion, but Lora didn't seem to mind.

"He's a good man," she said, blushing enough I had a rather uncharitable thought I quashed immediately. "He and Davis have been best friends since college. I've known him almost as long." She hesitated then, like there was more to say, before clearing her throat and sitting back, drinking the rest of her hot tea quickly. "Thank you so much, Ms. Fleming," she said. "I needed that."

I reached forward on impulse and squeezed her hand, her startled look followed by a few more tears. What, she wasn't expecting empathy? Likely not. "If there's anything I can do," I said.

She flickered a smile and squeezed back before gaining her feet, draping her coat and scarf over her arm. "Thank you so much," she said. "Good night." I let her go, finishing my tea to the sound of her footfalls retreating, before sighing myself and looking down at my now confused pug. "What's gotten into you?"

She meow-yawned in response, cinnamon bun tail wriggling a moment. But if she had more to say, I couldn't decipher it.

"Fine," I said. "Bed, then, miss."

She trundled outside into the garden while I cleaned the dishes and put them away, waiting by the glass door when I was done. I was almost to my apartment door, the basement suite all mine and off limits to guests, when I noticed a blob of white on the floor near the stairs and sighed. I could have just left it, of course, but my sense of responsibility—retired sheriff not as much an influence on my work ethic as my former high school principal mother, and it showed—wouldn't let me put it off. I retrieved the soft, white hat and headed for the second floor and Lora's room, planning to hang it on the doorknob and not disturb her.

Except, as I reached her door, the sound of voices inside had me pause and cock my head to listen. Because I hadn't expected her to be with a gentleman caller, had I? Not at this time of night. Had me thinking those rather unkind thoughts about her and Adam Carson all over again, because it was his voice, no question, that joined hers even if the thick, wooden door masked the actual words they spoke.

CHAPTER SIX

It took me about ten seconds of pondering to make a decision about my next move. You can bet I hovered on the edge of wanting to know what was going on behind that closed door despite Crew's request I stay out of the case. Mind you, the leaps of conclusions I came to in that brief span of time had me judging the pair who fell silent long enough to drive me away from their privacy after leaving the hat as I'd intended, sending me downstairs to my apartment with the firm and controlled self-assurance I'd mind my own business.

That didn't keep me from tossing and turning part of the night, however, even the deeply sleeping Petunia groaning at the interruptions when I sighed heavily for the millionth time. My need to follow through on staying out of things while my inner busybody tormented me resulted in a restless night and grumpy morning that I had to drown in a river of coffee just to manage to rise and shine enough to face my day.

The Jones sisters offered their nods and good mornings, the two-packs-a-day even though she didn't smoke gravel of Mary's deep voice filling the gap where her quiet sister, Betty, barely whispered. Not that it mattered to me, though the fact the elderly ladies had their own rigid and resistant rules as to what they would and would not do meant I was the one carrying breakfast offerings into the dining room while Betty rolled out a selection of hearty items as her sister trundled off to clean the carriage house across the garden. I waved off Daisy's attempt to help with the service, leaving her to chat with our outgoing guests—her favorite—and handled the grunt work myself.

I did my best not to watch for signs that Lora Zaine and Adam Carson had spent the night together, though their obvious avoidance of each other waved a giant red flag that made them look about as guilty of having an affair as anything I'd ever witnessed. I kept my peace as the other guests I hosted devoured their share of the breakfast spread before checking out, leaving the four as the only residents. At least, until check-in at 3PM.

Hopefully, this would all be over by then and I'd have my B&B back.

I kept my speculations to myself, but it was my

encounter with Jamie Myles as I returned from the koi pond, fish food for Fat Benny and his crew in one hand, that had me stop and listen despite myself. "I'm telling you I'll get you the money." He sounded angry, anxious, voice low and harsh, his back turned to me where he stood tucked behind one of the large bushes Grandmother Iris had cultivated in her distinctly English-style garden. If he thought standing there gave him privacy, however, he was sorely mistaken. "I know, but something came up." He half-turned as he spoke, finally catching sight of me, face blanching white before he muttered, "I'll call you back." Jamie hung up without a word to me and hurried off, tucking his phone into his pocket, leaving me to trail after him while resisting the urge to pursue him and ask what was up.

Because if I knew one thing? Money was an excellent motive where murder was concerned. Yes, I know, don't give me a hard time. There was no proof that I heard of Davis had been killed. Dr. Aberstock's blunt force trauma? Could easily have been caused by a slip and fall, icy patches on pavement in mountain towns in October hardly a newsworthy item. Not to mention a far cry from a criminal act. And for all I knew, Jamie's money conversation had nothing to do with his friend's death.

The thing about coincidences, though? I didn't believe in them even a little bit.

I was almost to the kitchen door, ready to carry on with my day and put aside any inkling of investigation, when the sound of voices lured me, groaning internally over my lack of ability to say no to that impulse, to the far side of the garden near the tall fence between Petunia's and the house next door, where a bench sat amid the flowers and Lora and Mac Dillon sat talking.

"You're sure the policy is up to date?" Lora seemed quite concerned about that.

"Yes, of course," he told her, patting her hand. "I saw to it personally, Lora. Davis might have abandoned you, but I made sure you'll be well taken care of."

That was an odd way to put things, wasn't it? As for Lora, she seemed relieved, not a hint of grief remaining. Had these two plotted to kill her ex-husband for the insurance money? Or had Mac acted alone on some imaginary premise Lora was into him?

Wait, was she playing *all* the friends?

The sound of a footfall behind me turned me with a gasp, clutching the canister of fish food to my chest in surprise, the sound of the dried bits rattling inside the cardboard loud in my ears. Crew Turner stood behind me, blue eyes flickering to the talking pair before he raised an eyebrow at me.

"Ms. Fleming," he said, so dry I felt the air pucker. He didn't have to use that tone.

"Sheriff." I stepped aside as Lora and Mac noticed us, both rising to join us when Crew gestured for them to do so.

"I have an update," he said to them. "If you'll follow me."

They did while I trailed along after the trio, drifting through the kitchen and to the doorway of my dining room which, it turned out, the sheriff who wanted me to mind my business had the audacity to claim for his little meeting of the minds.

Contrary creature. Grumble.

Well, if he was going to play this game with me and expect me to fall in line, he had another Fleming coming. Which meant, as the foursome sat and Crew addressed them, I took it upon myself to serve coffee while the sheriff glowered but didn't have the nerve to ask me to leave.

Instead, he squared those broad shoulders, serious expression a mix of compassion and professionalism, big hands on his narrow hips straining the uniform shirt across his muscular chest.

And I needed to stop staring before I spilled coffee on myself.

"I'm very sorry to tell you, Mrs. Zaine," he said, "but we have reason to believe your ex-husband was murdered." I knew it. Yikes, was that a smirk of satisfaction I had to quash before the widow noticed? Yes, yes it was.

I was a very bad person, but I was also right, so there.

"But who would have done such a thing?" Lora wept into one of my new white napkins while I winced over the lipstick and mascara stains. I'd have to bleach it for sure and that was so hard on the fibers.

Fiona Fleming. *Focus.*

"I don't have that answer yet," he said, meeting each of their gazes individually. Was it just me, or did all three men look incredibly uncomfortable and more than a little guilty?

Adam Carson pulled himself together the fastest, reaching out to hold Lora's hand. "I'm sure whatever happened, none of us had anything to do with it."

"Mr. Zaine was struck with a broken section of the parking lot's border," Crew said in that same tone of voice.

"So, it could have been an accident," Adam said, frowning at the sheriff. "I thought you told us it was murder?"

"Unfortunately," Crew said, "the body was found nowhere near where the blow was struck and with sufficient evidence, the body was then dragged from the edge of the lot to the car you arrived in, I can only draw one conclusion."

I didn't argue with him. Out loud, I mean. Because inside my head? I was having a lovely counter-point conversation. Even as the foursome broke out in protests about their involvement.

Crew silenced them with a wave of one hand. "I'm continuing my investigation," he said, "which means you're all to remain in Reading until I say otherwise."

"I'm calling my lawyer," Mac muttered.

"An excellent idea, Mr. Dillon," Crew said without batting those long, dark eyelashes of his. "I recommend you all do so before I question you. Now, if you'll excuse me." He strode from the room, and I followed because I couldn't help myself, could I?

"Crew." I stopped him at the door, saw (rather than heard) him sigh, those big shoulders bowing a little before he turned to face me. I'd closed the distance a bit too aggressively, the tall sheriff now towering over me with those deep, blue eyes only inches above mine, one of his hands on the doorknob, the other at his hip as he leaned forward and waited with a silent expression for me to go on. Which only made things worse, truth be told, because how could a man smell that freaking delicious while glaring frustrated irritation at me?

De. Freaking. *Licious.*

That's why the following conversation came out in blurty bits and pieces of the things I'd seen and heard as Crew's jaw tightened visibly and I finally rambled to a stop with a question.

"What if Davis fell and hit his head then crawled his way to the car?" There had to be a reason Crew thought it was murder.

He heaved a sigh for real this time, shaking his head. Then laughed, to my surprise, though it was a bit of a hopeless little sound that startled me. His free hand rose to run over his face before he let out a long, deep breath, amusement in his eyes but pained, so pained. "Fiona Fleming," he said. Paused, looked away with a soft tsking sound, then pulled the door open and me through it with him, closing it behind us. I found myself on my front porch with the handsome sheriff even closer to me, voice low and graveled as he spoke. "Of course, that's probably what happened. But I need to know otherwise." Wait, what? He watched understanding dawn on my face before nodding. "I'm shaking them up to see what falls out. There are enough questions in this whole mess I want to be sure I don't overlook anything." I nodded at that, feeling suddenly ridiculous. He was an excellent cop, I knew that. His FBI career now behind him, there was nothing about Crew Turner that suggested the man was an idiot.

"I get it," I said. "Sorry." No wonder he was annoyed with me.

Crew's expression relaxed. "You're in a unique position," he said with no small measure of resignation, "and I know I put you in it sending the suspects here. But I wanted them close. It would be too easy for them to make a quiet exit from the lodge." White Valley Ski Lodge was far enough up that mountain I understood his reasons. "That's not an invitation to get in the way, Fee." Crew hesitated one more moment before groaning like he was in pain then tossed his hands. "If you hear anything else…" He didn't finish, leaving me there in the wake of his scent and close proximity and emotional turmoil, heading for the street and his sheriff's pickup, driving off while I caught my breath and headed back inside.

Petunia sat just on the other side of the door, looking up at me in startled concern. Normally, she'd have just hung out with Daisy, but my best friend had left to run some errands. Before I could apologize for my sudden departure (without her, heaven forbid) the sound of shouting from the dining room caught my attention and had me hurrying to see what was going on.

To find Lora Zaine pointing a finger at all three men who stood in a semi-circle around her. "I know one of you did it," she shouted. "Which one of you killed my husband?"

CHAPTER SEVEN

"You're insane," Jamie spluttered, looking back and forth between Lora and his two friends. "We all know you've been sleeping with Adam." Well, that confirmed that, didn't it? Though the pained look on Mac's face had me wondering. "I had nothing to do with any of this and I can't believe I'm even in this mess." He sat abruptly, face pale, hand reflexively clutching at his phone. "I need to get back to the city." Yup, that was anxiety on the verge of panic, so maybe Jamie's money problems had nothing to do with Davis.

That left the other three, though, didn't it?

"My relationship with Adam is none of your business," Lora snarled. "And I'll have you know it didn't start until after Davis left me. So, you can

51

point your accusations elsewhere, Jamie Myles."

Mac's disappointment flashed across his face. "You two?" He wiped at his mouth with one shaking hand, sinking down next to Jamie, the hurt in his eyes making me wince. "You're really together?"

Lora hesitated, regret more fed by worry than empathy, though, since she hurried to him and wrung her hands like she now regretted speaking up. "It doesn't change how I feel about you, Mac."

Playing them all for fools, was she?

"I can't believe this," Jamie said, surging to his feet. "You have no idea what you've done."

"I can guess," Adam growled at him. "I'm well aware Davis backed out of your deal, Mac." The other man flinched, flushing while his bald friend's face contracted in anger. "Did you kill him over money?"

"You have no idea," Jamie snarled in return. "You've never had to worry about a thing a day in your life, Adam. You were born into money. The rest of us have to work for it. Not that you care."

"I care," Adam shot back. "Especially if it means you killed him."

"I didn't do anything of the sort," Jamie said, the other three now watching him with anger and accusation. "He told me he was done, fine. I can get other investors. But he could have at least given me time to find someone." Jamie's panic rose to the surface, the man's hands balled into fists at his sides, the one holding his phone clutching it so hard I feared he might break the fragile screen. "Instead, he tells me last night. Last night!" Jamie tossed his hands then, fists thudding against his hips as they fell, a choking laugh angrier and more frustrated than amused bursting from his trembling lips. "He knew I needed the funding by Monday."

"People have killed for less," Mac growled at him, turning his obvious hurt over Lora's betrayal on his friend like a feral animal looking for someone new to attack.

Jamie spun on him, finger jabbing in the other man's direction, startling Mac enough that he pulled back from the shaking index pointed in his face. "You should talk," he said. "Davis filled me in on more than his decision to back out on my project. Tell me, Mac, was he moving all of his investments from your control because he knew you were in love with Lora or because you're under investigation for embezzling money from your firm?"

Adam gaped while Lora's gasp of surprise had Mac spluttering, though I doubted it was the declaration of the man's affections that had them doing so.

Jamie wasn't done, turning to Lora then who looked up at him with a trembling lower lip and hurt on her face. "He knew about the life insurance policy," he said, throwing those words at her like weapons. I watched each of them land with flinch after flinch while Jamie went on in relentless fury. "You think he forgot about it? He was planning to cancel it. But he didn't get the chance, did he?" He backed away from Lora, heading for the exit to the hallway, not even noticing me while I huddled in the entrance observing the collective meltdown. "I'm done here," he said. "You can all fight it out over Davis and his money if you want. I have a business to save." And then he was gone, storming up the steps and finally slamming his door, the sound echoing down from the third floor while the other three sat in grim silence, staring at one another.

Accusations aside, I had a feeling the relationships in that room were about to become strained enough to end a lifetime of friendship.

They split and went their separate ways in silence, Adam striding out, Lora slinking from the room with her head down. Mac lingered a moment before hustling out himself, none of them meeting my eyes and leaving me to clean the dining room and ponder.

All four had access, motive and opportunity, that much was certain. Part of me wanted to write off Jamie at this point if only because he seemed to be the only one who appeared determined to move on. With the possibility that Davis Zaine had died of a perfectly innocent fall lingering in my mind, I could only carry on with my day and hope Crew had better luck than I did.

Because if one of the four had killed Davis? There was an excellent chance they'd get away with it without a solid bit of evidence to the contrary.

As for the sheriff, he seemed to be taking his good old time, though no lawyers made appearances while the four not-so-friends waited for him to speak to them directly. When I found Jamie Myles sitting in the garden, it was Petunia who made the first move, whatever reticence my dog had toward the foursome not applying to him, apparently. She huffed her waddling way to sit at his feet, distracting him from his sad and distant stare into nowhere with a grumbling request for attention. He reacted immediately, bending to rub her ears while she leaned enthusiastically into his hand.

I sat next to him with a smile. "She loves that," I said.

He flashed me a happier expression of his own as he lifted her to the bench between us. Petunia flopped against him and sat back so he could rub her belly while the man sighed.

"Dogs are the best," he said with great sadness in his voice, the emotion pulling down the corners of his mouth, though he didn't lose his willingness to give her the attention she desired. "If only people were so good."

I nodded. "They can be frustrating, especially when you care about them." Jamie let out a little laugh of agreement. "Have Lora and Adam always been a thing?"

"No," he said. "Lora was faithful despite Davis's issues. I know Mac always had a thing for her, Adam, too, but when Davis had his mid-life crisis, I figured she'd end up with one or the other of them."

So, it wasn't news. That meant the gasp had been about the insurance policy.

"I'm so sorry to hear about your business," I said. He shrugged. "That's what I get for asking a friend for money. I should have looked for other investors, but Davis assured me he was in."

"What changed his mind?" Jamie seemed amenable to the question despite my internal wince I'd pushed too far.

"Who knows with Davis?" He sat back then, Petunia dropping her head in his lap with a soft groan as he continued to rub her ears. "You know, we were all supposed to have it all worked out by now." I felt for him because I'd been in a similar state of mind not so long ago. "Instead, I'm divorced, I never see my kids and my business is tanking. And Davis is dead." He shook his head. "This was meant to be a fun weekend, a chance to get away and forget about the mess I've made of my own life. A reunion, kind of, since we've all drifted apart over the years. Instead, I'm just reminded that life really isn't fair and no matter what I do I'm never going to get ahead." Wow, that was defeatist, though I had my moments of self-doubt and flagellation during my breakup recovery. "If Adam hadn't paid for everything, I wouldn't have come at all."

Adam? "Not Davis?"

"Davis was too much of a tightwad," Jamie said. "Adam's old money, used to throw it around all the time. Still does, I guess." He exhaled long and slow and shaking. "Whatever. It doesn't matter." He looked down at my pug whose huge, dark eyes stared lovingly back. "I didn't kill him, you know."

I hadn't expected him to say that and, caught off guard, I didn't respond to his statement. "I'm sure the sheriff will let you leave soon," I said instead. "Please, if you need anything, don't hesitate." I stood, Petunia heaving herself up and hopping down with a grunt, following me as I left Jamie to his thoughts. If anything, our talk had pushed me into the not guilty arena, though I'd not always had the best badguydar in the past.

One thing was certain, Adam Carson didn't seem to have a motive. No money problems, he'd waited until Lora was free before pursuing her and it seemed like he genuinely cared for Davis regardless.

That left Mac. But when I went on a hunt for the man, he was nowhere to be found. Which meant I was going to leave it alone. Do my job. Mind my beeswax.

Right?

Yeah, right.

CHAPTER EIGHT

I wanted to stay out of it, I swear. But when I went down to my apartment for a quick break, I found myself on the sofa with my laptop balanced on a pillow across my thighs, Petunia snoring at my side, while I dug into the people staying under my roof.

With Daisy taking care of errands, I really should have been cleaning, though Mary and the two new girls I'd hired had that in hand and I'd already sorted out my bills and the new bookings, so I had an hour to myself. A normal person likely would have read a book, taken a walk or even a well-earned nap in that time. Me? I chose to investigate a murder I was supposed to stay out of.

Classic Fiona Fleming right there.

It didn't take long to find evidence of Jamie

Myles's financial insecurity, his small startup company developing new kinds of solar panels, led headlines in trade papers and magazines. The press was terrible, his attempt to take his company public tanking before it began. The one article featuring him and Davis Zaine stated the latter was investing in R&D, only to be negated six months later—just yesterday, in fact—with Davis dropping support and the magazine's writer claiming Jamie's company was as much as defunct.

It had to have hit hard. My former decision to write Jamie off as a suspect vanished in the face of such a humiliating experience. Surely, with all the drinks they'd imbibed the night before, it wouldn't have taken much of a temper tantrum and shoving match to turn into a slip, fall and blunt force trauma. If Jamie had confronted Davis and left him for dead, it was still possible the victim dragged himself to his car looking for help and simply didn't make it.

Manslaughter wasn't murder, but it was still illegal.

Adam Carson was old money, just like Jamie had said, his family's wealth that kind of mind-boggling ridiculousness that had me shaking my head and sighing over the dangers of excessive capitalism. If they were good friends, why wouldn't Adam help Jamie out? Then again, why did I care? The odds of such an arrangement having anything to do with Davis's death were slim to nope.

As for Mac Dillon, I didn't find anything about the supposed investigation into him for possible fraud and embezzlement which meant either Jamie had been mistaken or nothing had been decided yet. The investment firm where Mac worked was reputable enough, however, so if he was stealing from them, I had no doubt the truth would come out. But what connection could that have to Davis's death? Unless Davis knew and had evidence against him? I was reaching now and sighed as I searched the last person in the group.

Lora Zaine had kept her married name and popped up here and there in a few social columns in the Montpelier dailies. It looked like her family was rather wealthy too, so despite her fury over their finances, I couldn't imagine she was in trouble for money. Then again, why was she so concerned about the life insurance policy? And what had Mac to do with it if he was an investment broker? A bit more digging into him revealed the truth—he had a side hustle as an insurance agent, pretty recent, too, it seemed. Had he and Lora cooked up some means to benefit from Davis's death and followed through in a way they thought would look like an accident?

I closed my laptop in frustration, with enough questions swirling I barely paid attention as I climbed the steps to the main floor with Petunia following along at her waddling fastest, not realizing one of the focuses of my busy brain was descending the stairs until I almost ran into Mac Dillon.

"How's your room?" I blurted that question before I could stop myself, the hope I could engage him in conversation as I had Jamie dashed when he glared down at me like I was a bug under his shoe. Gone was his overdone flirting, replaced with arrogance I could almost feel.

"Adequate," he said, pushing past me and heading for the dining room. I scowled after him, partly for the lack of enthusiasm about my lovely place—he had one of the nicest rooms—and partly with the ingrained frustration that often arose when I wasn't taken seriously. Which meant I followed him, seeing him take a seat at one of the tables with his head down over his phone.

No way was he ignoring me. "Coffee, Mr. Dillon?" I brought the pot and a mug, while he grunted his agreement. "I understand you're an investment broker and insurance agent." Might as well lay it all out. He glanced up, frown still in place. But his interest sparked an idea that had me blurting on without even trying to stop. "I know it's terrible timing, but I don't suppose you'd have a second to advise me?"

As I suspected, I'd spoken the magic words. Mac instantly perked, his attitude shifting to a more open and friendly one. He kicked the chair beside his, pushing it out across my hardwood floor with a sound that had my teeth grinding. "Have a seat."

I perched there, pouring us both a cup, while the quiet hum of the house carried on around us, Mac setting his phone aside to lean toward me.

"What did you want to know?" He fished a card out of his pocket and handed it to me, his main investing job imprinted on the front, insurance information on the back. I looked up as he carried on speaking in a practiced tone that told me his spiel was well rehearsed and delivered. "You're at the perfect age to start saving, and this place is an excellent source of revenue for investment, I'm sure. Not to mention the fact while someone of your age likely hasn't considered life insurance, taking out a policy on yourself as a business owner makes excellent financial sense."

"I'm sure," I said, unwilling to admit he was right, and the thought hadn't crossed my mind. In fact, I'd been grateful just to make a go of things, to be honest, not considering the future and assuming it would take care of itself. But he was correct, I really did need to start planning for the decades ahead. Later. Right now, I had questions I couldn't shake.

"Have you thought about taking out a loan on this place to invest in an aggressive investment portfolio?" He reached for his phone again. "I can show you some excellent growth packages that would produce exciting dividends in a very short time."

"That sounds risky," I said, wrinkling my nose and digging deep for the silly woman who didn't know a thing about investing or money (while wishing it was a deeper hole rather than so shallow, yikes). "I was just talking to Jamie. His business is in trouble, isn't it? Because of investing?" Okay, yes, I was slathering it on thicker than cold honey in a snowstorm, but Mac bought it, every drop.

"Jamie's problem isn't investing," he said, "but concept. He's a startup and competition is fierce.

Maybe if he was more original..." he shrugged. "I was glad when Davis took my advice and backed out." He looked up then, lips tightening before he glanced my way like he worried we'd be overheard. "And he's trying to launch something. You're already established."

"I see," I said. But that was all I managed to say. I caught the footfalls approaching and barely had time to rise and turn as Jamie Myles flew past me and lunged for Mac, the pair grappling with one another immediately.

"How dare you?" Jamie's rage turned to an attempted punch that Mac blocked while I stared, open-mouthed and not sure what to do as the pair backpedaled away from the table, Jamie jerking on Mac's collar so hard it tore with a terrible sound.

"Davis deserved the truth!" Mac tried to pull himself free, but Jamie wasn't done, another blow swung and this one landing firmly under the other man's ribs. Mac's breath whooshed out of him as he doubled over, just as Adam Carson hurried in, getting between them, Lora hovering at my elbow with both hands over her open mouth, tears trickling down her cheeks.

"Enough. Enough!" Adam shoved them apart, supporting the still gasping Mac while Jamie panted his fury, hands still fisted in front of him.

"You betrayed me," he snarled.

"I *advised* him," Mac shot back. "I did my *job*."

"How could you do this to me?" Jamie tossed his hands, face contorting, while Adam stayed between them, one hand on Mac's arm, the other held out to Jamie. Mac drew a groaning breath and straightened, sinking into the chair he'd stood from when Jamie attacked, Lora circling past me to go to the injured man while Jamie glared at Adam. "Stay out of this."

"I won't," Adam said, low and firm. "It wasn't personal, Jamie. It was business. We all agreed a long time ago we wouldn't mix the two."

Jamie vibrated with pent-up anger, red splotches appearing on his face and neck, eyes narrowed to tight slits. "Said the man who never had to work for a dime in his life." He spun and stalked to the exit, turning at the last moment. "I thought it was Davis, now I know better."

"You killed the wrong person, is that it?" Mac wheezed the question while Lora gasped softly.

Jamie's expression stiffened, eyes flying wide as he looked back and forth between the widow and his two friends. "No, that's not... I didn't kill anyone."

"I said *enough*." Adam held out his hand to Lora who took it, before assisting Mac to his feet. "Let's get calmed down and have a civilized discussion when this is over. None of us are in the right emotional state to deal with this right now. Agreed?"

Jamie made a strangling noise but seemed to obey, leaving the room immediately, while Lora assisted Mac toward the door. Adam paused next to me with a regretful grimace, one hand settling gently on my elbow, though he dropped his touch instantly as though unsure of its welcome.

"I'm so sorry about this, Ms. Fleming," he said.

"I hope no damage was done. If so, I'm happy to cover any expenses."

I waved off his offer. "Do you think Jamie could have done it?"

He hesitated, then sighed deeply, shrugging. "I was hoping you could supply dinner for the four of us for tonight," he said. "I don't imagine the sheriff will want us wandering the streets of your lovely little town."

We didn't normally do dinner, but it had been on my list of things to try so I nodded.

"Of course," I said.

"Thank you, Ms. Fleming." Adam left me then, though he, too, stopped at the door, turning toward me. "There was a time when I would have said no, unquestioningly." To what? Then understanding hit me as he finished answering my question. "Now? I honestly don't know what any of us are capable of." He left with his head down and shoulders sagged while I watched him go and wondered.

CHAPTER NINE

Despite Adam's request, only two people came down for supper, the rest of my newly arrived guests out and about while I served him and Lora an early private meal in the dining room. I still had an hour before I had to be at Mom and Dad's for my own birthday meal, so I took full advantage of the time allotted to snoop on the couple.

Honestly? I'm not sure what I was expecting, but I was disappointed, nonetheless. They were as subdued as one would expect after a death, without the celebratory chicanery of a pair of lovers who'd succeeded in eliminating a problem, so I felt myself softening toward them while I personally handled their dinner.

"Thank you so much," Lora said as I topped up

her glass of wine when Adam slipped away to answer a phone call. She grasped my wrist, fingertips digging into my skin, her long, French manicure gone, making her own hands look small and fragile. "You must think I'm just a horrible person after the talk we had last night."

"Not at all," I said, nestling the bottle in the bowl of ice I'd improvised on the table. Petunia had been relegated to remain in the kitchen so she wouldn't be underfoot, though I knew she was more than happy to hang out with Mary and beg for scraps, so I didn't feel guilty. "You don't get to choose who you love." I grimaced a little at that, thinking about my own ex and what an idiot I'd been.

"You're right about that, Ms. Fleming." Adam had rejoined us without my noticing, sitting across from Lora, smiling sadly at her while she reached over and took his offered hand. "I've loved Lora since we met in college, but she was with Davis, and I never made a single move toward her. Not until he decided to give up the greatest prize in his life."

Lora blushed a little. "It doesn't keep both of us from feeling guilty," she said. "Even though we didn't do anything wrong."

"Why did you come to Reading, Lora?" She had to have known, even if Davis hadn't died so suddenly, her appearance wouldn't go over well.

"He was the father of my children," she said somewhat stiffly, sitting back, frown pulling the lines around her mouth. "He had a responsibility. I just wanted him to support his kids, that's all."

"I'm more than happy to do that, my dear," Adam said in a sweet voice.

"You shouldn't have to." She shook her head. "And now, you won't." Lora's chin came up as she met my eyes. "Davis's life insurance will be split evenly between them. Only they will benefit from his death where they couldn't from his life."

Sounded fair to me. Though what lengths would a mother go to when it came to protecting her children, I wondered?

"Did Davis know you two were in love?" Wow, Fee, just come out and ask already, why don't you?

But neither of them seemed to mind, Adam nodding in response. "As I told the sheriff," he said, "we were still friends despite everything. He knew neither of us acted on our feelings, that it was his choice. He seemed content with it. I've known Mac, Jamie and Davis for most of my life, Ms. Fleming. I don't want to lose that connection. I have so few I can count on."

And probably lost two along with the dead guy, but I wasn't going there at the moment. "Let me know if you need anything." I slipped from the room and left them to eat, though neither of them had removed themselves from my list of suspects. Okay, Crew's suspects, but stop quibbling a minute and hear me out. Momma Bear protecting her kids versus the rich friend who finally had what he wanted and the motive to want to keep that love safe?

I made a decision as I entered the kitchen, gesturing to one of my new staff (Shirley? Carla?

Yikes) to take over for me, Daisy done for the day, as I harnessed up my pug and headed for the front door and my coat.

But not to go to Mom and Dad's, not just yet. I still had time, didn't I, to make terrible life choices of the snooping variety? In all seriousness, I knew far more than I should have at this point and while I could have kept it all to myself, my dog needed walking before dinner, right? Not my fault the sheriff's office was on her usual route.

Oh, he was going to be *so* happy to see me.

CHAPTER TEN

To my surprise, Crew guided me into his office, through the bullpen and past Robert's glaring leer, closing his door behind us while Petunia sat and huffed up at him in expectation. The fact he always gave her attention and focus when she asked never failed to soften my heart to him, the big sheriff crouching to ruffle her ears and give her a nice, long ear scratch. The view from above was about as magnificent as one could imagine, the slight peek down his shirt revealing a hairless chest, the whorl of dark curls at his crown almost boyish, his scent carrying to me in a heady way that had me sweating in my wool coat within moments.

When he straightened to meet my eyes, his were soft around the edges, but guarded, like he knew why

I was there. When I opened my mouth to pour out what I knew in my willy-nilly fashion, he waved off my attempt.

"In a minute," he said. "You're not the only one coming to talk to me and you might as well hear what he has to say."

I blinked at that, no less surprised when a soft knock at the door revealed Dr. Aberstock. The portly, smiling ME entered at Crew's welcome, my favorite doctor grinning at me as he joined us.

"Fiona!" He reached out and squeezed my hands. "Happy birthday."

I blushed, I couldn't stop it, grinning back as he hugged me. "Thanks, Dr. Aberstock," I said, not even glancing Crew's way.

"Have a giant piece of Lucy's amazing chocolate cake for me, would you?" The doctor slapped his round belly with a laugh. "If Bernice wasn't such a good cook, I'd envy your father, Fee." His bright blue eyes turned to Crew. "You don't know what you're missing."

Crew's tight answering smile ended in a headshake. "I've partaken," he said, the mysteriousness of that suggestion making me frown. Mom made him a cake? When? Why? "You said you wanted to deliver your autopsy report personally."

Dr. Aberstock grunted a little. "All work and no play, my boy." He sighed then. "I found gravel embedded in Mr. Zaine's palms and under his nails, suggesting he did, in fact, drag himself across the parking lot. The blow to his head was a clean one, single impact, and there were no other distinguishing marks or damage to the body to suggest anything but a slip and fall." He slipped his gloves out of his jacket pocket and slapped them against his thigh. "Unless you have reason to believe otherwise, Crew, I'm calling this one an accident."

Crew nodded in response while I felt my entire body unclench. All of the tension I'd been holding onto while pondering what I'd heard from my guests fell away with that pronouncement, though the sheriff didn't seem as relieved.

"Thank you, doc," he said. "Have a great night."

Dr. Aberstock hugged me again before leaving, offering Petunia a soft pat on the way out. I hesitated despite myself, Crew staring down at the paperwork on his desk, frowning at it with one hand on his hip, fingers of his other splayed over the pages like he stood on the brink of something he couldn't shake.

"Do you think he's wrong?" I probably should have shut it and made an exit, but I couldn't bring myself to leave just yet. I trusted Dr. Aberstock completely but, like my dad, Crew had that look of a man whose gut told him otherwise and I couldn't discount it.

The sheriff looked up, his deep blue eyes unreadable. "I don't know," he said. "But without evidence, an accident it is. Good night, Ms. Fleming."

I left then, knowing a dismissal when I heard one, without filling him in on what I'd overheard, because what was the point now? I had about a half hour before I had to be at Mom and Dad's for dinner, so I let Petunia finish her walk, though as we neared the Harp and Thorne, I had a thought and, frowning over my apparent lack of ability to let things go that was probably inherited from Dad, I circled the building to the parking lot and headed for the edge of the pavement.

It wasn't hard to find the spot where Davis Zaine had fallen, the chunk of asphalt edging cut out and removed thanks to the Reading Sheriff's Department. I crouched with Petunia next to me, staring at the gap like it might reveal some magical information only to finally sigh when my pug meow-yawned her annoyance at our lack of motion, shuffling her feet beside me in boredom.

"I know, sweet girl," I said. "I'm dumb. Let's go." I stood and turned, to find my pug had wandered to the end of her leash and was snuffling something on the ground. Knowing her penchant for eating things that she shouldn't even to her physical detriment, I hurried to join her, snatching the item from her before she could swallow it.

Stared at it for a long moment with a frown deepening across my face while I caught my breath and looked up. The path to the place where I'd found Davis Zaine? Fell right in line with Petunia's find.

"Crew's going to be pissed," I said.

Petunia grinned in answer.

CHAPTER ELEVEN

Wouldn't you know, he wasn't at the office when I returned there? No way I was leaving what I found with Robert. My search continued, disappointed to find his truck wasn't parked out front of his little house a few streets over, either. I pondered what to do with the evidence I'd found and finally decided to head home and double-check my finding before I jumped to any conclusion I might regret.

That had me hurrying to Petunia's with my now-grumpy dog in tow, the pug's normally sauntering pace pushed to her limit. She followed me despite her weariness, harumphing her way up the steps one at a time while I slipped into the room in question.

I found the door open, the guest's possessions gone, likely relocated elsewhere, and I knew where. A quick check of the garbage in the bathroom told me the girls hadn't been in to clean yet and that the evidence in my pocket was a perfect match for the contents of the trash.

I straightened from the comparison, realizing I'd been handling proof of, if not murder, at least manslaughter and that Crew would be furious with me for tampering with evidence. I was, however, unaware until the last moment when I turned to leave, preparing to call him and alert him to the truth, that the previous occupant of the room had followed me inside.

It was Petunia's low grunt of welcome that told me I wasn't alone, though the normally sweet dog didn't rush forward to ask Lora Zaine for attention, instead sitting firmly on my feet with her head down and her ears flat back. She'd encountered an untrustworthy person not so long ago, a person who'd hurt her and tried to kill me. I could only imagine her sixth sense had somehow been triggered by the widow who faced me down with her hands shaking and rage crossing her face.

"Yours, I presume." I held out the fake French nail to show her, the one I found on the asphalt in her ex-husband's dragging path.

She snarled at me, the sound making goosebumps crawl up my spine. "You should have just stopped meddling," she said. "Davis is dead. Why couldn't you let it go?"

"You thought you could make it look like an accident," I said, circling her, trying to protect

Petunia who refused to listen, keeping herself between me and the shaking woman. I backed into the hallway, Lora following me. She didn't have a weapon, so I don't know why fear plunged icy daggers into my stomach. But there was something about the way she advanced on me, hands in claws at her sides, that terrified me. I had to get out of there and call Crew.

"You have no idea," she snarled. "What that man put me through. Yes, I followed him outside, we fought. I pushed him. He slipped." She shrugged like it was no big deal, mouth twisted in disgust. "He hit his head. I walked away." She looked down at her fingers. "I didn't realize until afterward, I'd lost a nail." Lora glared at the one in my hand. "You just had to ruin everything."

"Lora!" I heard Adam's gasp of her name, looked over my shoulder to find him ascending the steps toward us, face sheet white. He'd clearly heard her confession.

"It's not fair!" Her wail of fury had me turning back, but not in time to act.

I wasn't expecting her to lunge at me. I had no idea what her endgame might have been, but when I felt my heel catch on the top step and slow-motion acknowledged her hurtling form coming toward me with her face in a mask of rage and hate, I realized too late what her intentions were and that pushing her enemies to their deaths was the only weapon Lora Zaine needed.

All but for Petunia, my darling pug. She leaped up

at the last moment, head-butting Lora's knee, the woman staggering in surprise at the blow. I spun sideways while, keening in surprise, she lost her balance and tumbled headfirst down the stairs toward the foyer and into the shocked and horrified arms of Adam Carson.

I crouched, shaking and hugging my pug who licked my face with a soft whine of worry.

"All good, sweet girl," I whispered to her, tears stinging my eyes. "Thanks for the rescue."

She farted loudly before snorting all over me. For once, I couldn't care less.

CHAPTER TWELVE

I stood to one side, trying my best not to look like I was hugging myself for comfort and failing miserably, as Robert led the cuffed and defeated Lora Zaine out the front door of Petunia's. Crew hovered nearby, almost protective while the three men watched their former friend's ex-wife being led away. Adam Carson's pained expression had me shuddering, especially when he approached, the sheriff firmly placing himself between us.

"Ms. Fleming," Adam said, "I'm so very sorry for all of this."

I nodded, waving off his concern even as Daisy rushed through the front door of Petunia's, my parents on her heels, Mom and Dad both bypassing my former guests and joining me and Crew while

Adam, Mac and Jamie pulled back.

I was very late for my birthday dinner.

"Let me take care of this," Crew growled at me, gaze locked on the trio. "You're sure you're all right?" Those deep, blue eyes met mine and I found I couldn't breathe for a second.

Broke the trance I was in thanks to Mom's hand on my arm. "I'm okay," I said. "Petunia saved the day." I smiled shakily down at my pug who grinned her delight up at me. "Just get them out of my house, okay?"

Crew nodded and left me to my loving friend and family, Daisy's hug so tight I almost gasped, no match for Mom's squeeze of worry and Dad's bear-hug following.

"You sure you're all right, kid?" My gruff and stoic father usually managed to grin his way through even the roughest outcomes, but his worry for me wasn't one of those things he managed well.

"I will be." I heard the front door open, turned to see Crew escorting the men out.

"The FBI have some questions for you, Mr. Dillon," the sheriff said, confirming Jamie's accusation against his friend, it seemed. The sullen expression on Mac's face should have satisfied me, but it didn't.

I watched them all go, luggage in hand, and exhaled a sigh of relief. "Remind me that love isn't worth it?"

"Fiona Iris Fleming." Mom spun me toward her, my daily physical reminder I was going to age like a boss meeting my green eyes with her own, matching red hair threaded with the barest bits of shining silver, but lovely face firm. "Love absolutely *is*. The *right* love." She turned to Dad and touched his face with such tenderness I had to clear my throat from the emotional swell that followed. Reading's tall, broad-shouldered former sheriff had a solid foot of height on her, but she always managed to bring him to his knees somehow. Dad beamed at her and kissed her forehead before doing the same to mine and then, without a moment of hesitation, kissed Daisy, too. Then, his arms wrapped around all three of us and hugged us to him while Crew returned.

I couldn't decipher his expression when he paused to take in the Fleming collective. Was that regret? Resentment? Longing? Whatever the case, he nodded to Dad before doing the same to Mom.

"I'm sorry to say, but Lora Zaine will probably get off because her ex-husband's death was ultimately an accident." He didn't sound happy, matching his words, but she was out of my life and my bed and breakfast, and I was already feeling better. "It's up to the state's attorney if they decide to go for manslaughter."

"Thank you, Crew," Dad said.

"Of course." He nodded again, turned toward the door. Then spun back, meeting my eyes. "I'm happy you're okay, Fee." And left, boots making a heavy sound on the porch and steps before the door could close behind him.

"That boy," Mom said, tsking softly.

"I know," Daisy beamed at her, blinking tears.

"What?" I looked back and forth between them before glancing up at Dad.

Who shrugged, letting us all go. "Don't look at me," he laughed. "Now," he rubbed both big hands together in a rasping sound, "your mother has made her epic brisket and I'd hate to let it sit in the oven too long."

"And cake." She flashed me a smile. "Daisy, you're coming for dinner?"

My bestie nodded immediately. "Oh!" She hurried to the sidebar, pulling open a drawer and retrieving a small bag, handing it to me. "I forgot to give you your present."

I opened it, past the lovely pink heart paper and retrieved the dark green angora sweater I instantly hugged to me. "I'm wearing it to dinner."

She embraced me with a kiss on my cheek. "I'm so glad you're all right. I'll see you at the house!" Day waved and breezed out, but not before I caught more tears in her eyes.

Mom and Dad waited for me at the door, Petunia in her harness, ready to waddle her way the few blocks to the house where I grew up, while I raced downstairs to don the gorgeous sweater my best friend bought me. The fabric made me shiver and I grinned at my reflection, wondering what Crew would think of me in it. Before shrugging and laughing at myself.

The moment I reached the first floor, Mom handed me a box with Jacobs Flowers imprinted on it, the scent of roses from our local flower shop emerging even before I slipped off the cover and gasped at the stunning collection of dark red buds inside.

"You have a fan," Dad winked at Mom who batted at him.

"Read the card," she said, eyes twinkling, meaning she already had.

I slipped it open and stared in surprise at the message, not to mention the signature.

Thanks for the help, it read. *Happy birthday, Fee. Crew.*

So, he'd been buying me flowers when I went looking for him with evidence? How very fitting.

I looked up from the card with a little sigh that had me wriggling inside. Maybe Mom was right. The right love might make all the difference.

Right now? Life was about cake. And family. I followed my parents out the door of Petunia's, my shero pug at my side, and did my best not to wonder about local sheriffs and mixed messages and my penchant for dead bodies.

Turning twenty-nine—or any age—in Reading, Vermont?

I'd take it.

Looking for more Fiona Fleming? There's another novella now available! Go get **Deck the Halls and Murder**, for sale now!

FIONA FLEMING COZY MYSTERY NOVELLA

DECK THE HALLS AND MURDER

PATTI LARSEN

ABOUT THE AUTHOR

Everything you need to know about me is in this one statement: I've wanted to be a writer since I was a little girl, and now I'm doing it. How cool is that, being able to follow your dream and make it reality? I've tried everything from university to college, graduating the second with a journalism diploma (I sucked at telling real stories), am an enthusiastic improv performer (if you've never tried it, I highly recommend making things up as you go along as often as possible). I've even been in a Celtic girl band (some of our stuff is on YouTube!) and was an independent filmmaker (go check out the Lovely Witches Club). My life has been one creative thing after another—all leading me here, to writing books for a living.

Now with multiple series in happy publication, I live on beautiful and magical Prince Edward Island (I know you've heard of Anne of Green Gables) with my multitude of pets.

I love-love-love hearing from you! You can reach me (and I promise you, I'll always message back) at patti@pattilarsen.com. And if you're eager for your next dose of Patti Larsen books (usually about one release a month) come join my mailing list! All the best up and coming, giveaways, contests and, of course, my observations on the world (aren't you just dying to know what I think about everything?) all in one place: http://bit.ly/PattiLarsenEmail.

Last—but not least!—I hope you enjoyed what you read! Your happiness is my happiness. And I'd love to hear just what you thought. A review where you found this book would mean the world to me—reviews feed writers more than you will ever know. So, loved it (or not so much), your honest review would make my day. Thank you!